I0634130

Alice In Queerland

A Re-Education Fable

Karlyn Borysenko

RED
MENACE
PRESS

redmenacepress.com

Copyright © 2025 by Karlyn Borysenko

All rights reserved.

No portion of this book may be reproduced in any form without written permission from the publisher or author, except as permitted by U.S. copyright law.

First Edition: June 2025

This is a work of fiction. Names, characters, places, and incidents either are the products of the author's imagination or are used fictitiously. Any resemblance to actual persons, living or dead, businesses, companies, events, or locales is entirely coincidental.

This work is inspired by Lewis Carroll's "Alice's Adventures in Wonderland" (1865) and "Through the Looking-Glass" (1871), which are in the public domain.

Published by Red Menace Press
redmenacepress.com

Join the Red Menace Collective to support future works like this.
redmenacecollective.com

Contents

Dedication

To my second favorite Queer Marxist, ME O'Brien (they/them).

*ME's work has been critical to my understanding of
Queer Marxism. I can't thank they/them enough.*

I can't think of a better tribute to they/them than this satire.

*And yes, I'm aware they/them blocked me on BlueSky. And yes,
they/them made a whole public declaration encouraging everyone
else to block me too. But that just proves how powerful satire is.*

I see you, ME. I affirm your existence. Even if you wish I didn't.

Chapter 1

Down the Pronoun Hole

Alice had always been a curious girl. Not in the obnoxious way that got other kids labeled "disruptive," but the sort of curiosity that asked too many questions in the wrong rooms. She liked definitions. She liked boundaries. She liked knowing that words meant things.

Her phone buzzed against her leg. Dinah. Again.

"mandatory healing circle after school. you coming?"

Alice stared at the text, her thumb hovering over the keyboard. Six months ago, Dinah would have been texting about their math homework or sending memes about their physics teacher's weird habit of talking to the whiteboard. They'd been friends since third grade, back when friendship meant sharing fruit snacks and arguing about Pokemon cards.

"can't make it," Alice typed back.

The response was immediate: "that's literally violence."

Alice almost laughed. Almost. But Dinah wasn't joking anymore. Nothing was a joke anymore.

Which made school difficult.

Alice was in eighth grade now, thirteen years old and already feeling ancient. She'd watched her middle school transform year by year, policy by policy. By the time she reached eighth grade, she'd already sat through six mandatory assemblies on "inclusive language," watched a PowerPoint about microaggressions featuring cartoon vegetables, and been issued three different pronoun badges, none of which she'd asked for.

"Who can tell me about the causes of World War I?" Mr. Peterson asked from the front of the room. Last week, his email signature had changed to Mx. Peterson. The week before that, he'd removed the American flag from his desk and replaced it with a progress pride flag that had so many stripes Alice had lost count.

Alice knew the answer. She'd spent hours on her paper about the assassination of Archduke Ferdinand, the web of alliances, the powder keg of European tensions. Her hand twitched upward, then froze.

"Remember," Mx. Peterson added, his eyes scanning the room, "to consider how your positionality affects your interpretation of history."

Sarah, who now went by Sasha and wore buttons that said "they/them" and "destroy the binary," raised their hand. "I think we need to acknowledge that 'World War' is a Eurocentric term that centers Western conflicts while erasing indigenous struggles globally."

"Excellent critical analysis, Sasha!" Mx. Peterson nodded enthusiastically, making a note on his tablet. "You're really interrogating the dominant narrative. Extra credit for everyone who can find similar examples of linguistic imperialism in our textbook."

Alice's hand dropped to her desk. Last week, she'd been told her essay on the Industrial Revolution was "complicit in capitalist narratives." The week before, her analysis of The Great Gatsby had been "too binary in its understanding of class dynamics."

She glanced at her notebook where she'd written: "Causes of WWI: 1) Assassination 2) Alliances 3) Imperialism 4) Militarism 5) Nationalism"

Below it, someone had stuck a Post-it note in purple ink: "This list is violence. -Your Accountability Buddy"

Alice didn't know who her "accountability buddy" was supposed to be. She suspected it was Morgan, who sat behind her and had a habit of photographing other students' notebooks "for evidence."

It wasn't always like this. She remembered first grade being normal, whatever that meant. People said boys were boys and girls were girls, and the weirdest thing that happened was Max Chen bringing a peanut butter sandwich on a no-nut day. But slowly, the world around her started warping. First came the posters: "Words Hurt." Then the rainbow flag. Then the daily reminders that her lived experience was inherently violent to others.

Her sister Hannah had graduated three years ago. "It wasn't like this when I was there," she'd said at Thanksgiving, frowning at Alice's description of the new policies. "We had Gay-Straight Alliance, sure, but this sounds..." She'd trailed off, unwilling to finish the sentence even in their own home.

The bell rang, jolting Alice back to the present. Students began packing up, the rustle of backpacks and chatter filling the room.

"Before you go," Mx. Peterson called out, "remember that tomorrow we're discussing how binary thinking contributed to colonialism. Please read the article I posted about non-binary identities in pre-colonial societies."

Alice stuffed her notebook into her backpack, careful to keep the "violence" Post-it hidden. She'd started collecting them, these little accusations. Her folder at home had seventeen now.

"Alice, wait up!"

She turned to see Dinah approaching, her purple hair freshly dyed, a new button on her denim jacket: "Abolish Normal."

"You sure you can't come to the healing circle?" Dinah asked, but her eyes were already suspicious. "Kai's going to lead us through an exercise about releasing cisheteropatriarchal programming."

"I have to help my mom with something," Alice lied.

Dinah's face tightened. "Your mom. Right." She said it like Alice's mother was a problem to be solved. "You know, avoiding these spaces is a form of privilege hoarding."

"I'm not hoarding anything..."

"That's exactly what someone with privilege would say." Dinah's voice had taken on that particular tone, the one that meant she was quoting something she'd seen on TikTok. "Maybe examine why you're so resistant to doing the work."

Before Alice could respond, Dinah swept away, joining a group of students who were all wearing matching "Be Gay, Do Crime" t-shirts. Alice watched her go, remembering the Dinah who used to stay up until 3:00 AM texting her about their shared *Doctor Who* theories.

That Dinah was gone. Or transformed. Or maybe—and this thought made Alice's stomach twist—maybe that Dinah had never really existed at all.

It was Tuesday. October 17th. 2:47 PM.

Alice would remember these details because they marked the moment everything changed.

"Before we end class," Mx. Peterson said, smoothing his "Teaching Is Political" lanyard, "does anyone have questions about identity formation in historical contexts?"

The words came out before Alice could stop them. Maybe it was exhaustion. Maybe it was the way Dinah had looked at her at lunch, like she was something contaminated. Maybe it was just the accumulation of months of confusion, of watching words twist and reshape until they meant nothing and everything at once.

"What is a woman?"

The classroom air froze mid-breath. Someone's pencil rolled off a desk and hit the floor with a crack like breaking bones.

She hadn't meant to say it out loud. But there it was, hanging in the air like a lit match in a room full of gasoline.

Jax, who identified as "voidgender" and carried a stuffed octopus named They/Them, clutched their desk. "I'm literally shaking right now."

"I…" Alice started, but her voice was drowned out.

"UNSAFE!" Morgan screamed, slamming the red button on their desk. The light above it began to pulse, casting the room in intervals of crimson. "UNSAFE! UNSAFE!"

Other students joined in. The chorus grew. Alice noticed some students weren't shouting. They were recording on their phones, their faces lit by the promise of viral content.

Mx. Peterson's face went through several expressions—surprise, concern, then something Alice couldn't read. "Why would you ask that?" His voice was very quiet.

"I just…" Alice faltered. The words felt thick in her mouth. "We talk about gender all the time, but nobody ever actually defines…"

"Definitions are violence," Sasha interrupted, standing up so fast their chair scraped against the floor. "You're literally committing violence right now."

"No, I'm not, I'm just asking…"

"'Just asking questions,'" someone else mocked. "Classic TERF rhetoric."

Alice didn't know what a TERF was, but from the way they said it, it sounded like something you could catch.

"Alice," Mx. Peterson said, his voice strained, "I think you need to visit the Reflection Suite."

"But I didn't do anything wrong."

"Impact over intent," the class chanted in unison, a call-and-response they'd learned in their first week. "Impact over intent."

The DEI liaison arrived within minutes. Mx. River wore a blazer covered in pride pins and carried a tablet that never stopped pinging. They looked at Alice with the kind of sympathy reserved for terminally ill patients.

"Come with me," they said gently. "We're going to get you the help you need."

As Alice gathered her things, she caught a glimpse of something in the window...or was it a reflection in the glass? For just a moment, she saw it clearly: a wide grin floating in the air, attached to nothing. No face, no body, just that unsettling smile full of too many teeth. It hung there like a crescent moon turned sideways, visible only in the corner of her eye.

Then came the voice, not heard but felt, like words made of smoke curling through her mind:

"Oh, my. What a delicious question. They really don't like those anymore, do they?"

Alice spun toward the window, but the grin was gone. Had it ever been there? The other students were still focused on their phones, recording her "violence." Only she had seen it. Only she had heard it.

She shivered, despite the warm classroom, and followed Mx. River out into the hall.

The Reflection Suite felt like a waiting room designed by someone who'd read about comfort but never experienced it. Soft lighting that made everyone look sickly. Beanbags that swallowed you whole. Lavender-scented air that was just wrong enough to keep you on edge. It wasn't an environment for thinking or feeling. It was an environment for being fixed.

A giant cardboard cutout of Judith Butler loomed over the space, clipboard in hand, smiling like a benevolent prison warden. The eyes seemed to follow Alice as she sat down. On the wall, a banner in rainbow colors declared: "Gender is a Journey, Not a Destination."

She sat there for twenty minutes, but it felt like an eternity. There was no clock, no sense of time, just the faint sound of the lavender diffuser pumping air that smelled almost sickly sweet. The softness of the room was like a blanket of control, making her feel calm in a way that was distinctly unnatural. Like the calm wasn't hers.

Finally, the door opened, and someone entered. Taylor (they/them) introduced themselves as the "Restorative Inclusion Specialist." They wore a lavender jumpsuit that matched the room, glitter eyeliner that caught the light, and platform sneakers with trans-flag laces. They handed Alice a laminated identity chart titled "Exploring Your Inner Fluidity."

"Would you like to journal about how your internalized cisnormativity might have made others feel unsafe?" Taylor asked, their voice bright but completely void of any real emotion. They were clearly reading from a script.

Alice didn't understand the question. Her mind raced. Internalized what? She opened her mouth to ask, but Taylor was already nodding sympathetically and placing a journal on the table in front of her.

"Take all the time you need," Taylor said, though their tone suggested Alice should take exactly the prescribed amount of time and no more. "Remember, this is a brave space, not a safe space. Growth requires discomfort."

Before Alice could say anything, Taylor left, leaving her in the sterile silence of the room, the smell of lavender filling the space like a memory that wouldn't fade.

It was then that Alice noticed the oddest thing.

Near the reflection pod, pacing nervously, was a small white rabbit, no taller than her knee, wearing fishnet stockings and a cropped "They/Them" tank top. The rabbit was clutching a clipboard, muttering under its breath about "inclusion audits" and "pronoun compliance forms."

"Oh dear, oh dear," the rabbit stammered, checking what appeared to be a smart watch on its fuzzy wrist, "I'm late for the Self-ID tribunal! The pronoun compliance forms are due in five minutes!"

Alice blinked hard. The rabbit was still there, now pulling papers from a messenger bag covered in buttons that said things like "Respect My Existence or Expect My Resistance" and "Pronouns Save Lives."

Without thinking, Alice stood up. The air around her buzzed with static, like something was about to happen. Something big. She didn't know what possessed her, but she followed the rabbit.

"Wait," she called out, her voice barely above a whisper.

The rabbit turned, its pink eyes widening. "You can see me? But you're not even on the approved ally list!" It clutched its clipboard tighter. "This is highly irregular. I'll have to file an incident report."

"I just...where are you going?"

The rabbit's nose twitched anxiously. "The tribunal, of course! Though if you're asking that, you clearly haven't done the required reading. Very problematic. Very." It began hopping toward the far wall. "No time to explain! The consequences for tardiness are severe!"

Alice followed, her feet moving of their own accord. The rabbit approached what looked like a solid wall, but as it got closer, a door appeared. Or maybe it had always been there, hidden behind perception.

She tiptoed past a sensory nook blasting lo-fi queer affirmations ("You are valid. You are enough. Your identity is revolutionary."), the soft hum of positivity not masking the growing tension inside her. She slipped through a janitor's closet marked "PRIVATE: Faculty Only" in Comic Sans, her breath quickening as the silence enveloped her.

Inside, the room felt wrong. Too still. Too clean. The floor felt like it was pressing back against her, holding her in place. The air, once full of the fake calm of lavender, now felt heavy. Her feet moved instinctively, like a moth drawn to an unsettling light.

And then she heard it.

The voice. Smooth. Warm. Familiar, though she couldn't place from where.

"Thank you for choosing progress. You are now leaving outdated frameworks behind."

She turned to face the doorway, but it was too late. The light shifted, slowly, then suddenly flickering from white to pink to something hotter. It felt like her very skin was burning, like the walls of the school were shrinking and suffocating her.

"Correction will now begin," the voice echoed.

Then, without warning, the floor beneath her feet dropped.

As she fell, Alice caught one last glimpse of something—that same grin from the classroom window, now fully formed, floating in the air like a crescent moon. This time, she could make out more: the faint outline of a face, striped fur that seemed to exist in several places at once, eyes that gleamed with ancient amusement.

"Down the rabbit hole," the Cheshire Cat's voice purred, clear and unmistakable now, amused and knowing. "Though these days, they prefer to call it 'entering a brave space.' Same fall, different labels."

And then there was only the rushing dark, and the sense that she was leaving one world behind for another, one where questions were crimes and confusion was the only certainty.

The last thing she heard before the darkness took her was the rabbit's panicked voice from somewhere above: "She didn't even sign the liability waiver!"

Chapter 2

The Workshop That Never Ends

- -

Alice fell through darkness that tasted like lavender and felt like static. Her stomach lurched, her hands grasped at nothing, and somewhere above or below she could still hear the rabbit's panicked muttering about liability forms.

Then, suddenly, her feet hit something soft.

The landing should have hurt, but instead she bounced gently, once, twice, before settling onto what felt like a gigantic marshmallow. She lay there for a moment, trying to catch her breath, trying to make sense of what had just happened. The Reflection Suite, the rabbit, the fall. It all felt like a dream, except her heart was still racing and her school uniform was still damp with nervous sweat.

For a moment, she wished desperately for her normal eighth-grade problems. Pop quizzes and cafeteria food seemed like paradise compared to whatever this was.

"You're late," a familiar voice squeaked.

Alice sat up. The white rabbit stood a few feet away, tapping its smart watch with increasing agitation. Its fishnet stockings had somehow remained perfectly intact despite what must have been the same fall.

"Late for what?" Alice asked, her voice hoarse.

"For everything! The orientation, the pronouns circle, the mandatory workshop!" The rabbit's pink eyes darted nervously. "Oh, this will definitely affect my inclusion metrics. Come on, come on!"

Alice stood, her legs shaky, and finally took in her surroundings. She wasn't in the school anymore. That much was certain. The ceiling above swirled with clouds in pride flag colors, shifting and reforming in hypnotic patterns. The walls seemed to breathe, expanding and contracting with a rhythm that made her dizzy.

Strange mushrooms dotted the landscape, some tiny, some enormous, all glowing faintly with an inner light that pulsed like heartbeats. One cluster near the wall seemed particularly bright, almost inviting.

"Where... where are we?" Alice asked.

"The Integration Corridor, obviously," the rabbit replied, already hopping ahead. "First stop for all new arrivals. Didn't you read the welcome packet?"

"What welcome packet? I just fell through a floor!"

The rabbit turned, its nose twitching with disapproval. "Well, that explains the confusion. Spontaneous allies never read the materials. Very problematic. We'll have to add remedial training to your schedule."

Alice had no choice but to follow. As she took her first step forward, the ground beneath her feet changed.

The path was made of rubber. Or maybe memory foam. It squished beneath her shoes, each step lighting up in pastel rainbow bursts that squeaked like affirmation buttons. The sound was nauseating. A chorus of tiny voices saying "valid!" with every footfall. She tried walking on her tiptoes, but the path seemed to sense her resistance and squeaked louder.

The air felt heavier now, thick and sweet like melted frosting, but also synthetic, like a pride parade air freshener. It clung to her skin, made her feel sticky, uneasy. The world around her had shifted again. This wasn't the hallway she had walked through moments before. The walls pulsed, breathing in sync with the environment, expanding and contracting like a living organism. Every breath she took felt monitored, like even the air was checking for compliance.

"Excuse me," Alice called to the rabbit, who was now several hops ahead. "But where exactly is this? I mean, I know I'm not in school anymore, but..."

The rabbit didn't slow down. "Questions imply doubt. Doubt implies resistance. Resistance implies violence. Do try to keep up, both physically and ideologically."

Alice hurried after the rabbit, her confusion growing with each step. The landscape around them was impossible. Trees shaped like lipstick tubes towered overhead, each one topped with a sparkling star. Their trunks gleamed in shades of metallics and neons. Some had small mirrors attached to their bark, reflecting distorted versions of Alice as she passed.

Butterflies fluttered by with pronoun pins attached to their wings. She watched one land on a nearby flower. The flower immediately changed color to match the butterfly's pins. Everything here seemed to shift based on proximity to identity markers.

Floating billboards danced across the sky, beaming out slogans that made Alice's head spin:

"Question Nothing. Embrace Everything."

"Compassion Requires Compliance."

"Safe Spaces Begin in Your Mind."

"Your Doubt Is Violence."

"Transform or Be Transformed."

"Don't stare at the affirmation boards too long," the rabbit warned without looking back. "They're designed for subliminal absorption. Very effective, but some people get stuck in loops."

Alice quickly looked away, but the slogans seemed burned into her retinas. She blinked hard, trying to clear her vision.

The rabbit was muttering again, words drifting back to Alice: "Not enough representation in the mushroom grove. Still waiting on the intersectionality audit. Need to file a report about the binary birds in sector seven."

"Binary birds?" Alice asked, despite herself.

"Cardinals," the rabbit said with disgust. "Insisting on their 'male' and 'female' plumage. Very outdated. Very harmful. We've tried re-education, but they're remarkably resistant."

They reached a dome-shaped building made of iridescent glass and bedazzled bricks. The surface shimmered like oil on water, reflecting rainbow patterns that seemed to move independently of any light source. The structure pulsed with an internal energy that made Alice's teeth ache.

At the entrance, a sign read:

"Intro to Gender Fluidity: A Foundational Module for All Recruits

Facilitated by: Mx. Prism (they/she/ze)

Content Warning: This space practices radical acceptance. Coherent thoughts may be challenged."

Alice hesitated. "I don't think I'm supposed to be here."

The rabbit stopped and turned, their eyes wide with something between impatience and excitement. "Nobody's supposed to be anywhere. That's the point. Assignment is violence. Now come on. You'll love Prism. Ze's been deconstructing binaries since before you were assigned."

"Assigned?"

"At birth," the rabbit clarified, as if this explained everything. "Very traumatic. But we're here to help you heal from that violence."

Before Alice could respond, the rabbit had hopped through the entrance. The door seemed to ripple as they passed through, like water disturbed by a stone. Alice stood frozen for a moment, looking back at the path they'd traveled. It was already changing, the footprint lights fading, the ground reshaping itself. There was no going back the way she came.

Above, in the swirling clouds, she caught a glimpse of that familiar grin. The Cheshire Cat materialized just enough to be seen, lounging on what looked like a cloud made of cotton candy.

"Fascinating curriculum they have here," the Cat mused, its voice drifting down like smoke. "They teach you to question everything except their questions. Very progressive. Very exclusive kind of inclusion."

"You!" Alice exclaimed. "You were at my school. What is this place?"

The Cat's grin widened. "This place? It's where questions go to die and answers come to multiply. Where up is problematic and down is relative. Where you can be anything except certain."

"That doesn't help at all," Alice said, frustrated.

"Help implies there's something wrong," the Cat purred. "Careful with that kind of thinking here. They have treatments for it."

With that, the Cat began to fade, starting with its tail and ending with its grin, which lingered a moment longer. "Enjoy the workshop. Do try to keep your thoughts unauthorized. It's much more entertaining that way."

Alice stood alone before the rippling door. From inside, she could hear a low hum of voices, not quite singing, not quite chanting. Something in between. Something that made her skin crawl and her mind feel fuzzy.

She took a deep breath and stepped through.

Inside, the atmosphere was even stranger than she'd imagined. The air itself seemed thick with glitter, each particle catching light that came from nowhere and everywhere at once. Rows of beanbag chairs were arranged in a semi-circle facing a projection screen that showed swirling patterns in constantly shifting colors. The room was bathed in soft pink light that seemed to pulse with its own heartbeat.

A hundred faces turned to look at her. Some were human, or mostly human. Others defied description. One child was wearing six nametags, each in a different color, each with different pronouns. They waved at her with a hand that shifted colors mid-gesture, like a chameleon having an identity crisis.

"New recruit!" someone called out. It might have been a person or might have been a sentient rainbow. It was hard to tell in the shifting light.

A floating blob of what looked like galaxy-colored jello bobbed over to her. "I'm genderqueer goo," it announced cheerfully. "Pronouns are optional but feelings are mandatory!"

Alice tried to step back but found herself gently guided to an empty beanbag by invisible hands. Or maybe it was just the air pressure. Everything here felt like gentle coercion.

"Just in time," the rabbit said, materializing beside her with a clipboard. "Mx. Prism is about to begin. Remember: participation is mandatory, questions are violence, and silence is also violence. Good luck!"

The lights dimmed further. From the center of the room, a figure emerged. No, emerged wasn't right. They seemed to assemble themselves from the light particles in the air, becoming more solid with each second. Mx. Prism was tall, radiant, and appeared to exist in several dimensions at once. Their form shimmered like oil on water, constantly shifting between states of being.

"Welcome, recruits!" Mx. Prism's voice echoed not just in the room but inside Alice's skull, like thoughts that weren't her own. "Today, we unlearn. Gender isn't real, and that's the only truth we accept."

The room erupted in applause. Not normal applause. This was synchronized, rhythmic, almost mechanical. Alice found her own hands moving to clap before she consciously decided to.

"Today's lesson," Mx. Prism continued, floating above the ground now, "is about the violence of certainty. Who can tell me why knowing yourself is harmful?"

Dozens of hands shot up. The child with six nametags practically vibrated with excitement.

"Because knowing implies not-knowing!" they shouted. "And that creates a binary!"

"Excellent," Mx. Prism beamed, and the room literally brightened with their approval. "And binaries are?"

"Violence!" the room chanted in unison.

Then Mx. Prism paused, their shimmer faltering for just a moment. "Violence," they repeated, but their voice sounded different. Smaller. "I used to think I knew what that word meant. When I was young, before my awakening, I thought violence was..." They trailed off, looking confused, almost lost.

The room held its breath. The rabbit's pen stopped scratching.

Then Mx. Prism's form solidified again, their professional smile snapping back into place like a rubber band. "But of course, that was just my internalized oppression speaking! Now, let's examine our worksheets!"

Alice felt a chill. For just a second, she'd seen something real underneath the performance. Something almost human.

A worksheet materialized on her lap. She looked down at it, blinking in confusion. The title read "My Binary Bias and Me: A Journey of Unbecoming."

The first line was already filled in, in handwriting that looked eerily like her own: "I was socialized in cisheteronormative violence. I commit to embracing fluidity, uncertainty, and aesthetic revolution."

"But I didn't write this," Alice said aloud.

The room went silent. Every head turned to her. Even the floating lights seemed to pause in their dance.

"Didn't," Mx. Prism said slowly, as if tasting the word, "implies a binary between did and didn't. Very concerning."

Alice looked at the worksheet again. More words were appearing, writing themselves across the page:

"I will center non-linear narratives."

"I reject object permanence in selfhood."

"I apologize for my attachment to structure."

Her hands trembled as she held the paper. Around her, others had begun to recite from their worksheets, their voices blending into a hypnotic drone:

"Identity is performance. Performance is liberation."

"Gender is a spectrum and mine is evolving."

"Certainty is violence. Change is care."

The last phrase repeated endlessly, like a skipping record. Alice felt the words trying to worm their way into her brain, to replace her own thoughts. The lavender scent grew stronger, mixed with something else now. Something that made thinking feel like swimming through syrup.

She stood up abruptly. The beanbag made a wounded sound as she left it.

"I'm just... Alice," she said, her voice sounding small in the vast space. "I'm just Alice."

The chanting stopped. The temperature in the room seemed to drop ten degrees. One beanbag actually deflated with a long, sad hiss. Somewhere in the distance, a balloon popped.

"Just?" Mx. Prism tilted their head, and their neck kept tilting until it was at an impossible angle. Their smile never wavered, but something behind their eyes went cold. "Just implies limitation. Limitation implies definition. Definition implies violence."

"Everything can't be violence," Alice protested. "If everything is violence, then nothing is."

A collective gasp rippled through the room. Someone whispered, "She's doing it again. The questioning thing."

The rabbit was scribbling furiously on their clipboard. "Second instance of non-compliance. Suggesting binary between violence and non-violence. Exhibiting dangerous levels of coherence."

Two towering figures materialized beside Alice. They wore what looked like medical scrubs made of fog, covered in pins and badges that changed slogans every few seconds. One held a clipboard labeled "Cognitive Realignment Intake." The other carried what appeared to be a sparkle-covered neural adjustment device.

"You're exhibiting signs of coherence," the first figure said, their voice like white noise. "Very concerning. Very treatable."

"Best to intervene early," the second agreed. "Before the certainty sets in permanently. We've seen what happens when ideological resistance calcifies. The subjects become completely unable to embrace their true fluid selves. They get stuck in the old world forever."

They reached for Alice's arms. Their touch was soft but inexorable, like being held by a ghost that had somehow learned to grip.

"Where are you taking me?" Alice asked, trying to pull away.

"Somewhere safe," one replied, their smile too wide for their face.

"For everyone," the other added.

As they guided her toward a door she hadn't noticed before, a familiar voice drifted through the air like smoke:

"Oh, don't struggle. It only makes the trial longer."

The Cheshire Cat materialized on top of a nearby bookshelf, examining its claws with theatrical disinterest. The two figures dragging Alice didn't seem to notice it at all. The Cat was more visible than before, its purple and pink stripes shifting like television static, its body partly there and partly somewhere else entirely.

"Trial?" Alice asked, her voice catching.

"Of course," the Cat purred, its grin widening until it seemed to take up more space than its face. "Did you think you could just ask questions without consequences? They have a whole system for this. Very efficient. Very just. Very much like a witch trial, but with better branding and more rainbow flags."

"Can't you help me?" Alice pleaded as the figures continued pulling her toward the door.

The Cat rolled onto its back, still floating above the bookshelf. "Help implies I'm on a side. I'm merely observing the experiment. Though I will say this..." It paused, one eye winking shut while the other grew impossibly large. "When they ask you to confess, remember: they already know you're guilty. The trial is just to determine of what."

"That doesn't make any sense!"

"Exactly," the Cat said, now hanging upside down from nothing at all. "You're starting to understand. The beauty of their system is that confusion is also a form of guilt. As is clarity. As is everything in between."

The Cat began grooming a paw that kept disappearing and reappearing. "Oh, and when they offer you the chance to apologize, don't. Apologies here are like quicksand. The more you struggle to make things right, the deeper you sink."

"Then what should I do?"

The Cat's grin tilted at an impossible angle. "Whatever you do will be wrong. That's the point. You've already committed the cardinal sin - you've noticed the game. Very rude of you, really."

The door they approached pulsed with soft pastel light. Above it, a sign blinked in and out of existence: "SAFE SPACE: AUTHORIZED THOUGHTS ONLY"

"I don't want to go in there," Alice said, digging her heels in.

"Want implies choice," the first figure said sadly. "Choice implies options. Options create hierarchies."

"Hierarchies are violence," the second figure concluded.

The Cheshire Cat floated down to Alice's eye level, its face serious for the first time. "One last thing. In there, they'll try to make you forget who you are. They're very good at it. Most people thank them afterwards." Its eyes gleamed with something that might have been respect. "But you asked what a woman is. That means you still remember that words used to mean things. Hold onto that. It's the only weapon you have."

Behind her, Alice could hear Mx. Prism resuming the lesson: "Now, let's explore how binary thinking led to colonialism, capitalism, and the invention of clocks!"

The figures pulled her through the doorway. The last thing she saw before the door closed was the Cheshire Cat's grin, but this time it wasn't smiling. It was baring its teeth.

"See you at the trial," its voice whispered, though its mouth didn't move. "Do try to put on a good show. They so very rarely get anyone who actually fights back. It's been ages since they've had to actually think."

Then the door shut with a soft, final click, and Alice found herself in a long, sterile corridor that smelled of judgment and lavender-scented conformity.

Chapter 3

The Trial of Thoughtcrime

T he corridor stretched before Alice like a throat waiting to swallow. Every few feet, motivational posters lined the walls, their messages growing more ominous the deeper she went:

"Your Microaggression Is Our Opportunity."

"Feelings Don't Care About Your Facts."

"Center Others by Erasing Yourself!"

"In This Space We Believe: Words Are Weapons, Silence Is Death, Questions Are Hate"

The two figures flanked her, their grip still soft but inescapable. Their badges caught the fluorescent light. Alice could now see their names: Justice (they/them) and Equity (xe/xir). They moved in perfect synchronization, like dancers who'd rehearsed this routine a thousand times.

"How long is this hallway?" Alice asked, her voice echoing off the walls.

"Distance is a colonial construct," Justice replied without looking at her.

"We prefer to think of it as a journey of indefinite length," Equity added.

Alice's stomach sank. She remembered what the Cheshire Cat had said about apologies being like quicksand. Already she could feel the urge to say sorry bubbling up in her throat, even though she wasn't sure what she'd be apologizing for.

The hallway finally ended at a set of double doors. These weren't the shimmering, magical portals she'd seen before. These were institutional gray, with wire-reinforced glass windows that revealed nothing but darkness beyond. Above them, words appeared and disappeared like a digital marquee:

"QUEER TRIBUNAL: THOUGHTCRIME COURT"
"JUSTICE IN PROGRESS"
"NO RECORDING DEVICES (UNLESS YOU'RE CREATING CONTENT)"

Justice and Equity pushed the doors open. The sound they made wasn't a creak but a sigh, as if the room itself was disappointed in Alice for requiring its services.

Inside was a courtroom unlike any she had ever seen. It looked like someone had crashed a TikTok convention into a Soviet show trial and decorated the wreckage with rainbow flags. The walls were lined with screens, each displaying a never-ending stream of vertical videos. Activists performed their trauma. Influencers sobbed about their journeys. The audio overlapped into white noise that sounded like a beehive having a panic attack.

At the center of the room, on a raised platform that pulsed with LED strips, sat the Queer Tribunal. Seven figures arranged in a semicircle, each one camera-ready and utterly terrifying in their performative authenticity.

The one in the center had a neon-blue buzz cut and cheekbones that could cut glass. They wore a judge's robe made entirely of pronoun pins that clinked when they moved. To their left sat someone in a dress made of printed tweets, the fabric constantly refreshing with new text. To their right, a person whose entire aesthetic seemed to be "sexy librarian meets revolution" shuffled through a deck of what looked like tarot cards but were actually printed Instagram stories.

"The accused will approach," the center judge said, never looking up from their phone. They were typing something, probably a post about this very moment.

Justice and Equity guided Alice to a spot marked with an X made of biodegradable glitter. A ring light suddenly blazed to life above her, making her squint.

"Better lighting for the documentation," someone explained.

A figure emerged from the shadows. They wore a suit jacket covered in certification badges: "Ally Level 9," "Completed Anti-Racism Training (Advanced)," "Pronouns: Any/All," "Certified Safe Space Creator." They cleared their throat with the gravity of someone about to perform Shakespeare.

"The accused stands before us bearing the weight of three distinct violations against our collective harmony," they began, their voice rising and falling like a practiced sermon. "First, in a space dedicated to learning and growth, Alice weaponized curiosity itself by asking 'What is a woman?', a question designed to destabilize and harm those still on their journeys of becoming.

"Second," they continued, pausing for effect, "when offered the gift of fluidity, the freedom to be anything and everything, she responded with aggressive simplicity. 'I'm just Alice,' she said, as if identity could be so cruelly singular, so violently fixed.

"And finally," their voice dropped to a whisper that somehow carried to every corner of the room, "she dared to suggest that our careful taxonomy of harm was somehow...illogical. That if everything is violence, then nothing is. Such unauthorized philosophy threatens the very foundations of our carefully constructed reality."

The tribunal gasped in unison, their hands flying to their chests in practiced shock. One of them, wearing false eyelashes so long they needed their own pronouns, fanned themselves with a program titled "Today's Agenda: Dismantling Alice."

"How does the accused identify?" the judge with the blue hair asked, finally looking up from their phone.

Alice straightened her shoulders. "I'm Alice," she said simply.

The temperature in the room seemed to drop. Someone's coffee cup actually cracked.

"Just Alice?" the judge asked, their voice dangerously sweet. "No qualifiers? No intersectional analysis? No acknowledgment of your positionality?"

"I don't know what my positionality is," Alice admitted. "I'm thirteen. I'm in eighth grade. I like reading and I'm good at math. Is that...positioning?"

The tribunal member with the tarot cards drew one and held it up. It showed a picture of a crying white woman. "The Karen of Cups," they intoned. "She resists enlightenment."

"I'm not resisting anything," Alice protested. "I just asked a question."

"Ah," said another tribunal member, this one wearing a cape made of progress flags. "The 'just asking questions' defense. Classic. Textbook. Practically vintage at this point."

They all turned to their phones, typing furiously. Alice could see her own image appearing on their screens, already filtered and captioned: "Privilege in Action: A Case Study."

The White Rabbit scurried up to the prosecutor's table, clipboard in hand, practically vibrating with excitement. "Excellent work!" it whispered loudly. "The documentation is perfect. I've already filed the preliminary reports and cross-referenced with the Problematic Behaviors Database. This case will make an excellent training module!"

It turned to beam at Alice with genuine enthusiasm. "You should feel honored! Your violation is so textbook it's going straight into the orientation materials. Future recruits will learn about the dangers of unauthorized questioning by studying your file!"

The rabbit's pink eyes sparkled with professional pride as it made another note on its clipboard. "I do so love it when the system works exactly as designed."

The prosecutor continued reading charges. "Furthermore, the accused demonstrated dangerous levels of coherence when she refused to accept that her worksheet was self-completing. She insisted on authorship, thereby perpetuating the myth of individual consciousness."

"Individual consciousness is colonial," someone muttered.

"How do you plead?" the center judge asked.

Alice remembered the Cheshire Cat's warning about apologies. "Not guilty," she said, her voice steadier than she felt.

The room erupted. Not in anger exactly, but in something worse. Disappointment. They looked at her the way her mother looked at burnt cookies. Fixable, but requiring effort.

"She doesn't understand," one tribunal member said sadly.

"The violence of her ignorance," another agreed.

"So young, yet so problematic."

The judge raised a hand for silence. The rings on their fingers caught the light like tiny disco balls. "Alice, do you understand why you're here?"

"Because I asked a question in class?"

"No," the judge said patiently, as if explaining to a very small child. "You're here because your question was an act of violence. Your confusion is violence. Your very existence in that space, asking that question, with your..." they gestured vaguely at all of Alice, "unexamined privilege, was an act of violence."

"But I didn't hurt anyone," Alice insisted.

The tribunal member with the Instagram tarot cards stood up dramatically. "Intent," they declared, "is irrelevant. Impact is everything. And your impact was devastating."

They pulled out their phone and showed a video. It was Alice in the classroom, asking her question. But the video had been edited. Dramatic music played. Zoom-ins on shocked faces. Crying emojis floated across the screen. The caption read: "CIS GIRL CHOOSES VIOLENCE: A THREAD"

"This has three million views," the tribunal member continued. "Do you know how many people you've literally killed with your words?"

"Killed?" Alice's voice cracked. "No one died!"

"Metaphorically killed," another tribunal member clarified. "Which is worse, because the victims have to live with it."

The prosecutor stepped forward again. "The state recommends immediate intervention. Full ideological reconstruction. Minimum six months of intensive allyship training."

"Six months?" Alice felt her knees go weak.

"You're lucky," the judge said. "We've seen cases like yours before. Young people corrupted by...what was it?" They consulted their phone. "Ah yes. 'Reading books without proper context warnings.' Very dangerous. But treatable, if caught early."

"I just wanted to know what words mean," Alice said, her voice small.

The tribunal exchanged knowing looks. One of them actually patted their heart in sympathy.

"Meaning," the judge said gently, "is not for you to determine. Meaning is communal. Meaning is consensus. Meaning is whatever we decide it is today, subject to change based on emerging discourse."

"But then how do we communicate?"

"Communication is overrated," the prosecutor interjected. "What matters is performance. Solidarity. Compliance."

The judge leaned forward, their voice taking on a therapeutic tone. "Alice, I'm going to give you one chance. One opportunity to show growth. All you have to do is apologize."

The room held its breath. Phones hovered, ready to record either her redemption or her downfall.

Alice thought of the Cheshire Cat's warning. Apologies here are like quicksand.

"Apologize for what?" she asked.

Wrong answer.

The tribunal erupted in perfectly synchronized disappointment. They shook their heads in unison, typed in unison, sighed in unison.

"She's not ready," the judge declared. "Take her to the Identity Reconstruction Center. Phase One: Pronoun Immersion Therapy."

Justice and Equity appeared at Alice's sides again. As they led her toward yet another door, Alice caught a glimpse of movement in the corner. A familiar grin, floating near the ceiling.

"Pride comes before a fall," the Cheshire Cat's voice whispered, meant only for her. "But in here, falling is the point. The question is: how far down does their rabbit hole go?"

The door opened to reveal not another corridor, but a small, windowless room. Chrome chairs with soft restraints. Screens on every surface. The smell of lavender so thick it made her eyes water.

"Don't worry," Equity said, guiding her to a chair. "Everyone finds their true self eventually."

"Some just take longer than others," Justice added. "But we have all the time in the world."

They left her there, in the soft, padded silence. Alice sat in the chrome chair, waiting for whatever came next. The screens around her stayed dark. The lavender scent seemed to pulse with her heartbeat.

She closed her eyes, trying to hold onto herself. Trying to remember what the Cheshire Cat had said about words meaning things.

Minutes passed. Or maybe hours. Time felt different here, stretched like taffy.

Then, just when she thought she might scream from the silence, she heard it. A soft click. She opened her eyes.

The door had opened by itself.

Not the door they'd brought her through. A different door, one she hadn't noticed before. Through it, she could smell something that wasn't lavender. Something sharp and sweet, like overripe fruit. Something that reminded her of the world before all this madness began.

She stood slowly, half-expecting alarms to sound. But there was only silence and that strange, inviting scent.

Alice took a step toward the door. Then another.

Whatever was through there couldn't be worse than chrome chairs and forced apologies.

Could it?

Chapter 4

The Forest of Endless Becoming

A lice stepped through the mysterious door, her heart still racing from the trial. The chrome and screens vanished behind her as if they'd never existed. She found herself in a forest unlike any she'd ever seen.

The air hit her first. It was sharp and sweet, like fruit left too long in the sun. It clung to her throat, making each breath feel like swallowing syrup. The trees were wrong. Their trunks were smooth as glass, silver like mirrors, but when Alice looked at them, her reflection kept changing. In one tree she was taller, in another her hair was short, in a third she couldn't see herself at all.

The ground beneath her feet wasn't quite solid. It shifted between moss and memory foam with each step, as if the forest floor couldn't decide what it wanted to be. Pink light filtered through the canopy, casting everything in the sickly glow of a fever dream.

Then she heard it. The whisper.

They/them...She/her...Xe/xem...We/they...

The pronouns drifted through the air like a chant, coming from the trees themselves. Each leaf seemed to murmur its own identity, creating a rustling cacophony of self-declaration.

"Where am I now?" Alice whispered to herself.

"You're in the Self-ID Forest, obviously," a voice replied.

Alice spun around. A figure stood by a sparkling river, but "stood" wasn't quite right. They flickered. One moment they were tall and willowy, wearing a flowing skirt, long hair cascading down their back. The next, they were short and angular, pixie-cut hair above a loose hoodie. They didn't just change clothes. They changed everything, constantly, like a human kaleidoscope.

"I'm Maya," the figure said, their voice shifting pitch with each word. "Or Max. Or Morgan. Depends on the moment. Right now I'm feeling very she/her, but ask me again in ten minutes." They smiled, and even their smile couldn't stay the same shape. "Are you here for the self-actualization journey?"

"I'm trying to find my way out," Alice said carefully.

Maya-Max-Morgan laughed, a sound like wind chimes in a tornado. "Out? Oh honey, the only way out is through. Through yourself. Through your old ideas. Through everything you thought you knew."

Alice watched, mesmerized and disturbed, as the figure's face rearranged itself mid-sentence. "But how do you...how do you know who you are?"

"That's the point!" they exclaimed, throwing arms that were sometimes thick, sometimes thin, into the air. "I don't! Isn't it wonderful? Every moment is a choice. Every breath is a new identity. I'm everything and nothing all at once."

Before Alice could respond, another figure emerged from between the silver trees. This one was tall, muscular, draped in flowing robes that seemed to be made of mist. They looked at Alice with an expression of profound disappointment.

"Cis-adjacent," they announced, as if diagnosing a disease.

"I'm sorry?" Alice said.

"Your energy. Your aura. The way you stand there so...certain." The figure's form flickered between presentations. Masculine, feminine, neither, both. "You still think you're something specific, don't you? How limiting."

"I think I'm Alice," she said, her voice smaller than she intended.

The figure actually shuddered. "Names. Another prison. I haven't used the same name twice in months." They began to walk away, then paused. "No wonder the forest feels so tense with you here. All that certainty is like...pollution."

They vanished mid-sentence, literally fading into the air, leaving Alice alone with the shape-shifting Maya-Max-Morgan.

"Don't mind them," Maya said, though they were now someone else entirely. "Some people are further along the journey. You'll get there. We all do, eventually."

Alice walked deeper into the forest, partly to escape the conversation, partly because standing still felt dangerous here. The ground might decide to swallow her if she stayed in one place too long.

The river beside her glowed faintly, its water warm and viscous. When she dipped her fingers in, the liquid clung to her skin like silver paint, leaving traces that whispered "they" and "them" before finally evaporating.

"Curious little thing, aren't you?"

The voice was deep, amused, and came from above. Alice looked up to see a massive caterpillar draped across a mushroom the size of a small house. But this wasn't like the caterpillars from her childhood books. This one had dozens of segments, each a different color, each with its own set of eyes. It was smoking something from a pipe that changed shape with every puff.

"I'm just trying to understand this place," Alice said.

"Understanding." The caterpillar savored the word like wine. "Such a binary concept. You understand or you don't. You know or you don't know. How terribly limiting."

Smoke poured from its many mouths, forming shapes in the air, symbols that almost meant something before dissolving into chaos.

"The others called me cis-adjacent," Alice said. "What does that even mean?"

The caterpillar laughed, a sound like gravel in a blender. "It means you still think you're something. Some fixed, stable thing. 'I'm Alice,' you say, as if that means anything. As if you're the same Alice who woke up this morning, or the same Alice who asked that dangerous question in class."

"But I am the same person," Alice protested.

"Are you?" The caterpillar's segments began to shift, each one rotating independently. "Every cell in your body replaces itself. Every thought is new. Every moment you're dying and being reborn. The only difference between you and us," it gestured with several arms toward the flickering figures in the forest, "is that we've accepted it. We've embraced the change."

"It looks exhausting," Alice said without thinking.

The caterpillar's many eyes narrowed. "What's exhausting is resistance. Fighting the flow. Clinging to outdated concepts like..." it shuddered dramatically, "consistency."

"But if everything changes all the time, how do you function? How do you have relationships? How do you do anything?"

"Function is fascist," the caterpillar replied smoothly. "Relationships are fluid contracts renegotiated moment by moment. And as for doing..." It took a long drag from its pipe. "Doing is just another form of being, and being is just another form of becoming."

Alice felt a headache forming. "That doesn't make any sense."

"Sense," the caterpillar mused, "is just another binary. Makes sense, doesn't make sense. You're still trapped in the old ways of thinking. But I can help you, if you're willing."

"Help me how?"

"Transform, of course. Real transformation, not the surface-level costume changes you see around here." The caterpillar leaned down, its faces coming uncomfortably close to Alice. "I can show you how to truly let go. To stop being Alice and start being...everything."

Alice looked around the forest. Figures flickered between the trees, their forms never stable, their voices a constant chorus of changing pronouns. The air itself seemed to shift, unable to decide what temperature it wanted to be.

"What if I don't want to be everything?" she asked quietly. "What if I just want to be me?"

The caterpillar reared back as if slapped. "Want? Want implies desire. Desire implies lack. Lack implies incompleteness. You're making this so much harder than it needs to be."

"Maybe because it shouldn't be this hard," Alice shot back, surprising herself with her anger. "Maybe being a person shouldn't require a philosophy degree and a complete rejection of reality."

The forest seemed to freeze. Even the flickering figures stopped mid-transformation. The caterpillar's many eyes blinked in sequence, like a very long, very judgmental wave.

"Reality," it said finally, "is just another construct. And a particularly violent one at that."

Before Alice could respond, the mushroom began to sink into the ground, taking the caterpillar with it. "When you're ready to evolve," it called out as it disappeared, "the forest will find you. It always does."

Alice stood alone among the silver trees, their whispered pronouns growing louder. She could feel the forest trying to work on her, trying to blur her edges, make her uncertain. Part of her wanted to give in. It would be so much easier to just...flow. To stop fighting. To let go of the exhausting business of being someone specific.

But then she remembered the Cheshire Cat's words: "Hold onto that. It's the only weapon you have."

She was Alice. She had asked what a woman was. She had refused to clap. She had said no to the worksheet. And she was still Alice.

The forest didn't like that. She could feel its displeasure in the way the ground became less stable beneath her feet, the way the air grew thicker, the way the whispers became more insistent.

But she kept walking, looking for something, anything, that stayed the same long enough to be real.

In the distance, she thought she saw a clearing. Or maybe it was just another illusion. In this place, it was impossible to tell.

But it was a direction, and that was more than she'd had since falling down the rabbit hole.

So Alice walked toward it, still stubbornly, defiantly, herself.

Chapter 5

Tea with the Academic Mob

A lice pushed through another cluster of silver trees, their whispered pronouns growing fainter behind her. She'd been walking for what felt like hours, though in a place where time might not exist, who could tell? Her feet ached, her throat was dry, and she was beginning to wonder if the forest went on forever when she heard it.

Laughter. The clink of china. Voices rising and falling in academic cadence.

She hesitated. Every encounter in this place had been a test, a trap, or a lecture. But the sound of teacups meant civilization of some kind. Maybe even sanity.

She should have known better.

The trees parted to reveal a clearing where impossibility had set up housekeeping. A table stretched across the space, long as a runway and twice as dramatic. It was set for dozens, maybe hundreds, each place setting deliberately mismatched. A Victorian teacup next to a mason jar, bone china beside recycled bamboo, silver spoons paired with plastic forks that proclaimed "Eating is Political!"

The tablecloth wasn't one fabric but hundreds, stitched together like a quilt made by someone who'd raided a protest supply closet. Alice could read fragments: "Silence = Death," "The Future is Fluid," "Decolonize Your Plate," "Utensils are a Western Construct."

And the guests. Oh, the guests.

They moved like a swarm of very educated bees, buzzing with theory, drunk on their own vocabulary. A procession of academics, activists, and influencers swirled around the table in choreographed chaos. Someone in a cape made entirely of peer-reviewed articles swept past. Another person wore a dress of living Twitter threads, the fabric scrolling with real-time hot takes.

At the head of it all sat the Mad Hatter.

Alice knew it was him before anyone said a word. He didn't just occupy space. He performed it. His outfit was a violation of every design principle ever conceived: a blazer stitched from pride flags, protest banners, and what looked like pages from Gender Trouble. His hat towered three feet above his head, an architectural impossibility decorated with buttons that cycled through slogans too fast to read. His glasses were unnecessary, thick enough to see through time, worn purely for the aesthetic of intelligence.

"Ah!" He rose as he spotted Alice, arms spreading wide like he was about to conduct a symphony. "Another lost soul, wandering in the forest of certainty! Come! Sit! We have so much to unteach you!"

Alice found herself pulled forward by hands that appeared from nowhere. Or maybe they'd always been there, waiting. Before she could protest, she was seated at the table, a teacup materializing in front of her. The liquid inside shifted from purple to green to something that didn't have a name.

"Welcome," the Mad Hatter said, sliding into the chair beside her with movement that defied physics, "to the Tea Party of Queer Thought, where time is a colonial construct and the only thing that matters is the eternal Now!"

"Time isn't a construct," Alice said, fatigue making her blunt. "My watch is still ticking."

The table gasped collectively, a sound like a hundred gender studies papers being clutched at once.

The Hatter's smile didn't waver, but his eyes glittered with the joy of someone who'd just found a teaching moment. "Oh, my dear binary child. Watches are just mechanical oppression! Little tyrants on your wrist, forcing you into the violence of schedules, the fascism of punctuality!"

He grabbed a pocket watch from his coat and held it up. The face had no numbers, just the word "NOW" written in every direction. "See? Fixed! Liberated! Free from the chronological hegemon!"

"But how do you know when to meet for tea?" Alice asked.

"We don't meet," a woman with a septum ring and pupils like dinner plates interjected. "We converge. We manifest. We appear when the universe requires our presence."

"She means we have a group chat," someone whispered, then yelped as multiple elbows found their ribs.

The Hatter poured tea from a pot that wasn't there into Alice's already full cup. The liquid didn't overflow. It simply existed in defiance of physics.

"Here, you can be anything. The clock has no hands. Time is a lie told by the oppressors to make you linear."

Alice stared. "Time...isn't real?"

"Not here," he replied. "Here, there is only Now. Now is freedom. Past and future are colonial constructs. The eternal Now is where your truest self can emerge."

Her watch was still ticking, but the second hand seemed to drag. Or loop. Or blink. She looked away.

"But...don't we need the past to understand where we came from? Don't we need a future to move toward?"

The Hatter frowned gently, like a parent indulging a child. "Oh, sweet child. That kind of thinking is what they programmed into you. The future is just another form of control. And the past? That's trauma in disguise. Let it all go. You must stop othering yourself with continuity."

Alice felt her thoughts beginning to blur at the edges. The rhythm of his words was hypnotic, almost sensible if she didn't think too hard about them.

"Tell me," the Hatter continued, his voice now reverent, "what brings you to our eternal non-temporal gathering?"

"I'm trying to find something real," Alice said. "Something that stays the same for more than five seconds."

The laughter that erupted wasn't cruel, exactly. It was worse. It was pitying.

"Real!" the Hatter exclaimed, wiping tears from his eyes. "Oh, you delicious little essentialist! Next you'll be telling us you believe in truth!"

"I do believe in truth," Alice said stubbornly.

The table erupted. Teacups rattled. Someone fainted into their phone, livestreaming their swoon. A person in a suit made of recycled theory papers began hyperventilating into a bag marked "Emergency Deconstruction Kit."

"Truth," the Hatter said, his voice dropping to a theatrical whisper, "is the most violent lie ever told. There is no truth, only competing narratives, intersecting experiences, multiplicities of meaning!"

"But surely some things are just true," Alice insisted. "Water is wet. Fire is hot. I'm sitting at this table."

"Are you though?" The Hatter's grin widened until it threatened to split his face. "Or is the table sitting at you? Is wetness a property of water, or is water a property of wetness? Is fire hot, or does hotness manifest as fire when observed through the oppressive lens of temperature?"

Alice's head spun. Around her, the other guests had begun their performance. Someone stood on their chair, reciting Judith Butler from memory but replacing every third word with "revolution." Another person was conducting a struggle session with the sugar cubes, demanding they acknowledge their role in colonialism.

"This is ridiculous," Alice muttered.

"Ridiculous is a judgment," the Hatter corrected. "Judgments are hierarchies. Hierarchies are violence. Therefore, you've just committed assault. More tea?"

He poured again, though her cup was still impossibly full. The liquid was now the color of confused rage.

"Listen," Alice said, trying to find solid ground in the conversation. "I understand that language can be complex, and meaning can shift, but surely we need some stable definitions to communicate..."

"COMMUNICATE?" The Hatter leaped onto the table, somehow not disturbing a single cup. "Communication assumes a speaker and a listener! It assumes meaning can be transferred! It assumes, it assumes, it ASSUMES!"

The other guests began chanting: "Assume nothing! Presume nothing! Know nothing! Be everything!"

Alice watched in horror as the chant grew louder, more rhythmic. The guests swayed in unison, their eyes glazing over. Someone bit into a scone and declared it "problematically binary" because it had a clear inside and outside.

"This is insane," Alice said.

"Sanity," the Hatter sang, now dancing between the cups with impossible grace, "is just consensus reality enforced by the psychiatric-industrial complex! Madness is freedom! Confusion is clarity! War is peace!"

"That's from 1984!" Alice shouted. "That's literally doublethink!"

The Hatter froze mid-pirouette. The entire table went silent. Even the self-stirring spoons stopped their autonomous labor.

"Did you just," the Hatter said slowly, "literally use 'literally'?"

"I..."

"And cite a white male author?"

"Orwell was criticizing..."

"WITHOUT A TRIGGER WARNING?"

The table exploded into motion. Guests leaped to their feet, pointing, gasping, reaching for their phones to document this act of literary violence. Someone started a Twitter thread in real-time. Another person began writing a grant proposal for studying the trauma of unexpected Orwell references.

"Seize her!" the Hatter commanded. "She's thinking in binaries! She's believing in authors! She's implying that words mean things!"

Hands reached for Alice from every direction. But she was already moving, adrenaline lending her speed. She grabbed the tablecloth and yanked, sending the impossible tea service crashing to the ground. Cups that defied physics shattered into very real pieces.

"MY DISSERTATION!" someone screamed, watching their edible thesis dissolve into the grass.

Alice ran, the sound of academic rage behind her. But as she reached the edge of the clearing, she heard the Hatter's voice, no longer theatrical, no longer performing:

"You can't run from theory, Alice. It's already inside you. Every word you speak has been theorized. Every thought you think has been problematized. We're not the mad ones here. You are, for thinking you can escape."

She turned back to see him standing alone at the ruined table, his costume suddenly looking less like armor and more like a prison made of other people's ideas.

"Maybe," she called back, "but at least my madness is my own."

Then she was in the trees again, running toward whatever came next, leaving the eternal tea party to its eternal performance.

Behind her, she could hear them rebuilding, resetting, preparing for the next lost soul to wander in. Because the show, like time itself in their twisted philosophy, must go now.

Always now.

Forever now.

Until now meant nothing at all.

Chapter 6

The Garden of Heartless Accountability

A lice ran until her lungs burned and her legs shook. The trees began to thin, their whispered pronouns fading to silence. She stumbled into a clearing and stopped, hands on her knees, gasping for breath.

When she looked up, her heart froze.

Before her stood a palace of impossible beauty, marble so white it hurt to look at, gold that caught light that didn't exist, gardens so perfect they looked embalmed. But it was the smell that made her stomach turn. Beneath the roses and lavender was something else. Iron. Meat. The smell of a butcher shop drowning in perfume.

The gates stood open. She could see figures moving in the garden beyond, but something was wrong with their silhouettes. They seemed to be carrying something. Holding something. Cradling something in their arms like broken dolls.

Alice stepped closer, and the world lurched.

The figures were headless. Each one walked the garden paths with perfect posture, tending roses with careful hands, their own severed heads tucked under their arms or held by the hair like lanterns. The heads never stopped moving. Lips forming words over and over: "I'm sorry. I'm so sorry. I should have listened. I'll do better. Please forgive me. I'm sorry."

One passed close enough for Alice to see its eyes, still blinking, still crying, still desperately trying to make contact with anyone who would look.

Alice found the White Rabbit kneeling beside one of the headless bodies, frantically checking its clipboard against the figure's name tag.

"This is wrong," the rabbit muttered, flipping through pages. "The paperwork says voluntary rehabilitation. Says subject showed excellent progress. Says..."

It looked up at the body's severed head, still mouthing apologies nearby. The head's lips moved silently: "I'm sorry, I'm sorry, I should have known better, I'm sorry..."

The rabbit's ears drooped. "You were supposed to get better," it whispered to the head. "The forms said you got better."

Alice backed away from the scene, her stomach churning.

She turned toward the palace entrance, and froze.

"Beautiful, aren't they?"

Alice spun around. The Queen stood behind her, and Alice's first thought was that this was what happened when drag became a weapon of war.

Queen Heartless towered in heels that could kill, her padding creating an hourglass silhouette that defied physics. The gown was a living thing made of screens showing final moments, mouths opening in last words, hands reaching up in supplication, eyes widening in realization. Her wig reached toward heaven in a platinum monument to excess, adorned with a crown of gold and bone.

But it was the face that made it clear. This was drag as ideology, drag as dominion. The makeup was applied with architectural precision: lips overdrawn into a permanent smile of condescension, contour sharp enough to cut glass, highlight visible from space, lashes so heavy they required effort to keep open. Every element of femininity exaggerated until it became a threat.

"Welcome to the Garden of Justice," Queen Heartless purred, her voice pitched in that particular theatrical register that drag queens used to command attention across a noisy bar, if the bar was a killing field. "I do hope you'll enjoy your stay. However brief it might be."

She glided forward with the practiced movement of someone who'd learned to walk in heels as a weapon, and Alice saw that her train was held by headless courtiers, their bodies moving in perfect choreography while their heads, balanced on their backs, continued their endless apologies.

"What is this place?" Alice whispered.

"This?" The Queen gestured grandly, every movement choreographed for maximum impact. "This is what accountability looks like, darling. This is a safe space. See how peaceful it is? How harmonious? No one argues anymore. No one questions. Everyone is exactly where they should be."

She paused by a rosebush where a figure knelt, carefully pruning with hands that shook. Its head sat beside it on the ground, tears streaming down its face as it whispered, "I should have known. The violence of my silence. I should have known."

"This one posted a question," the Queen explained conversationally, adjusting her breastplate with practiced ease. "Just a question, can you imagine? About whether intentions matter. Such violence. Such harm to the community. But look how much they've grown!"

The head's eyes found Alice, but its mouth was trapped in its apology loop. Only the eyes could plead.

"You killed them," Alice said, her voice barely a whisper.

"Killed?" Queen Heartless laughed, throwing her head back in that exaggerated way drag queens perfected, but the sound was like crystal breaking in a velvet glove. "Oh no, darling. Death would be abandonment. We keep them here. Part of the community forever. Contributing. Apologizing. Growing. Isn't that what justice looks like?"

She led Alice deeper into the garden, past fountains that ran red before the color shifted to pink, past hedges trimmed into the shape of raised fists, past flower beds where the headless bodies worked tirelessly, their heads lined up on the ground like spectators at their own degradation.

And then Alice saw it. The center of the garden. The heart of this nightmare.

A stage dominated the space, white marble stained with something that wouldn't wash out. At its center stood a guillotine, but not like any from history books. This one was decorated with rainbow ribbons, covered in glitter, its blade engraved with "Community Care" in flowing script. Around it, stadium seating rose in tiers, filled with hundreds of people holding phones, waiting.

"Ah," Queen Heartless said, checking a pocket watch made of someone's jaw while touching up her lipstick with the other hand. "Perfect timing. We have a trial in five minutes. Well, a retrial."

"A retrial?"

"Of course! We're not barbarians, darling. Everyone gets a fair trial. The community decides. Very democratic. Very just." She smiled, and her teeth were too white, too sharp, like veneers designed by someone who'd never seen a human smile. "The defendant wasn't sufficiently remorseful the first time. Kept insisting they had a 'point.' But don't worry, I'm sure they've learned better now. Haven't you, sweetness?"

The guards dragged someone onto the stage, a young person clutching their own head to their chest. The head was sobbing, but the body moved with mechanical precision, kneeling in the designated spot.

"Wait," Alice said. "They're already...how can you try them if they're already..."

"Oh, this is for insufficient growth," Queen Heartless explained, voguing slightly as she spoke, unable to resist the performance even now. "They apologized, yes, but did they MEAN it? The community thinks not."

The crowd roared approval. Someone started a wave. Others held up signs:

"The Community Sees All!"

"This Is A Harm-Free Zone!"

"Your Words Are Literally Killing Us!"

Queen Heartless took the stage, and the crowd fell silent. She raised her arms, and her dress of dying moments flickered faster. She was in her element now, a performer with the ultimate captive audience.

"Community! We gather here in love!" Her voice boomed with the power of someone used to projecting over bass lines and drunk bachelorettes.

"LOVE!" the crowd screamed back.

"We gather here for justice!"

"JUSTICE!"

"We gather here to protect the vulnerable!"

"PROTECT!"

"Now," the Queen said, suddenly gentle, maternal, touching her chest with Lee Press-On Nails that could gouge eyes, "our lost lamb here wrote…and I quote…'maybe we should consider nuance.' Nuance! Can you imagine? In this economy?"

The crowd booed. Someone threw a rainbow stress ball.

"But that's not all!" The Queen was building momentum now, working the crowd like a professional. "They also suggested...brace yourselves...that 'people can grow without being destroyed.'"

Gasps. Actual gasps. Someone clutched their chest and had to be fanned.

"So," Queen Heartless continued, smile never wavering, "what does the community say? Have they shown sufficient growth? Or do we need to help them grow... more?"

The answer was unanimous: "MORE! MORE! MORE!"

"The community has spoken!" The Queen clapped her hands in delight. "Bring the special blade!"

Guards appeared with something smaller, more delicate. Alice realized with horror it was designed for fingers. The headless person's body began to shake, but stayed kneeling. The head in their lap was whispering faster now: "I understand, I understand, I was wrong, I understand..."

"One finger for each problematic thought!" Queen Heartless announced cheerfully. "Who wants to count with me?"

The crowd cheered. The blade fell. Alice looked away, but she could hear it, the wet sound, the crowd counting "ONE! TWO! THREE!" like it was a game show.

"Beautiful!" The Queen wiped away a fake tear, careful not to smudge her makeup. "Such growth! Such accountability! Take them back to the garden. Next case!"

"Alice!"

She turned.

One of the headless figures had approached. She recognized the face. It was one of the shape-shifters from the forest, but now frozen in a single form.

"You have to run," the head mouthed silently while its lips kept forming apologies. "They're already talking about you. Someone saw you in the forest. Someone heard you at the tea party. You're trending."

Alice's phone—she'd forgotten she still had it—buzzed. She looked down. #AliceIsOverParty was already climbing. Her face, distorted by filters, appeared under headlines: "Dangerous Questioner Still At Large" and "Is Alice the New Face of Hate?"

On stage, Queen Heartless was already warming up for the next act. "Community! Do we have time for one more before dinner?"

"ALICE!" someone in the crowd screamed. "Alice is here! The girl who asked what a woman is!"

Every head turned. Every phone pivoted. The Queen's painted face lit up with genuine joy.

"Alice?" She peered into the crowd, one hand shading her eyes dramatically. "THE Alice? Oh, this is better than Christmas! Bring her up! Bring her up!"

The crowd surged toward her. Alice tried to run, but hands grabbed her from every direction. They dragged her toward the stage, phones in her face, voices screaming evidence:

"She asked what a woman is!"
"She said 'just Alice' like identity doesn't matter!"
"She refused to apologize at the workshop!"
"She said if everything is violence then nothing is!"
"She ruined the tea party!"
"She questioned the forest!"

They threw her onto the stage. Queen Heartless loomed over her, adjusting her wig with one hand while gesturing grandly with the other.

"Alice! Darling! So wonderful to finally meet you!" She turned to the crowd. "Isn't she exactly what you'd expect? Look at that defiant little face! That problematic certainty! Ladies, gentlemen, and everyone beyond and between...we have ourselves a LIVE ONE!"

The crowd went wild. Someone started selling "Alice is Cancelled" t-shirts. They came in all the colors of the Progress flag.

"Now then," Queen Heartless said, sitting on a throne that appeared from nowhere, crossing her legs with practiced elegance. "Let's review the evidence. Who has receipts?"

The crowd exploded. Everyone had receipts. Phones thrust forward showing screenshots, recordings, testimonies:

"She made my friend feel unsafe by existing!"

"She literally committed violence by asking questions!"

"My cousin's roommate's dog walker said she doesn't even have pronouns in her bio!"

"She probably reads books without checking if the authors are problematic!"

Queen Heartless nodded along, making sympathetic noises. "Terrible. Awful. Unforgivable. Alice, darling, what do you have to say for yourself?"

Alice stood up straight. The crowd fell silent, waiting.

"I asked a question because I wanted to understand."

"UNDERSTANDING IS GATEKEEPING!" someone screamed.

"I said I was 'just Alice' because that's my name."

"NAMES ARE COLONIAL!"

"I didn't apologize because I didn't do anything wrong."

The crowd lost it. Phones flew. Someone fainted. Queen Heartless had to fan herself with a program made of canceled people's last tweets.

"She... she said... she didn't do anything wrong?" The Queen's voice quavered with theatrical shock. "Did you all hear that? She doesn't think she did anything wrong!"

"OFF WITH HER HEAD!" The chant started immediately. "OFF WITH HER HEAD! OFF WITH HER HEAD!"

Queen Heartless raised a hand for silence. "Now, now. We must follow due process. Alice, this is your last chance. Will you apologize? Will you admit your violence? Will you submit to re-education? Will you let us fix you?"

Alice looked at the rainbow guillotine. At the crowd baying for blood. At the Queen smiling behind her makeup mask. At the headless bodies tending the gardens. At the heads that couldn't stop apologizing even after death.

"No," she said. "No, I won't. This isn't justice. It's a performance. You're not protecting anyone. You're just getting high on cruelty and calling it righteousness."

Queen Heartless's perfect face cracked. Her smile froze. For a moment, something raw and horrible showed through. Not anger, but need. The need to be righteous. The need to punish. The need to feel power while calling it love.

Then the mask slammed back into place.

"The community has spoken!" she shrieked, pointing one bedazzled nail at Alice. "OFF WITH HER HEAD!"

The guards rushed forward. The crowd pressed in. Alice was surrounded, hands reaching, voices screaming. They dragged her toward the rainbow guillotine. The crowd was chanting, counting down like it was New Year's Eve.

"TEN! NINE! EIGHT!"

A small white blur shot through the crowd toward Alice. The White Rabbit collided with the guards, its clipboard flying, papers scattering like snow. For once, it wasn't muttering about protocols or deadlines.

"SEVEN! SIX! FIVE!"

"Run!" the rabbit gasped, grabbing Alice's hand. "The hedge. There's a gap!" Its pink eyes were wild, but not with its usual panic. This was different. This was choice.

Alice stared at it. "But you work for them…"

"FOUR! THREE!"

The rabbit's whiskers trembled. "I brought you here," it said, its voice small but clear. "I brought all of them here. But I can't…I won't watch them take your head too."

"TWO!"

Guards were closing in from all sides. The rabbit shoved Alice toward a gap in the hedge she hadn't seen. "Go! Now!"

"What about you?"

The rabbit looked back at the rainbow guillotine, at Queen Heartless screaming orders, at the mob baying for blood. Then it looked at Alice one last time. "Just go," it whispered. "Please."

"ONE!"

Alice twisted free from the guards and dove toward the gap. The last thing she saw was the White Rabbit standing motionless in the chaos, tears streaming down its fur as Queen Heartless's eyes found it in the crowd.

"SHE'S ESCAPING!"

"GET HER!"

"WHO LET HER GO?"

"CHECK YOUR PHONES! WHO'S NEAREST?"

Alice ran through a maze of hedges, the sound of pursuit growing. She could hear Queen Heartless's voice rising above the chaos: "FIND HER! And find who helped her! We have a collaborator! CANCEL THEM ALL!"

The mob turned on itself. "It was you!" "No, you!" "Check everyone's posts!" "Who didn't chant loud enough?" Someone was already being dragged to the stage as Alice ran.

Dead end. A wall of thorns rose before her.

"Oh, this is disappointing. I did hope you'd last longer."

The Cheshire Cat materialized on top of the wall, but its usual grin was strained. "Still, you've made it further than most. They usually confess by now. Start apologizing. Beg to be rehabilitated."

"Help me," Alice gasped.

"Help?" The Cat's eyes gleamed. "I'm just a neutral observer. Though..." It glanced at the approaching mob. "I do hate a boring ending. Tell me, Alice. What did you learn here?"

"That they'll kill you for questioning them."

"Close. They'll kill you for making them question themselves. Much worse crime." The Cat's grin widened.

"The wall is an illusion, by the way. Their whole garden is. It only has power if you believe in its boundaries."

Alice heard the mob round the corner. Queen Heartless led them, her dress of final moments flickering like a snuff film ball gown, her wig slightly askew from the chase.

"There!" the Queen shrieked. "The violent questioner! The one who refuses to grow!"

Alice looked at the wall of thorns. Looked at the mob. Looked at the Cat, who was already fading.

"Just remember," its voice drifted, "in a world where words are violence, violence becomes words. Rather circular, don't you think?"

Alice didn't think. She ran straight at the wall of thorns.

And passed right through.

The screams of rage behind her were real enough. Queen Heartless's voice rose above them all: "Find her! Hunt her! She cannot be allowed to exist without judgment! The community demands justice! And someone check the garden, we have a traitor!"

But Alice was already gone, running into whatever new nightmare awaited, leaving behind the garden of heads that wouldn't stop apologizing and bodies that couldn't stop serving their own destruction.

Behind her, she could hear them returning to the stage. The show must go on. Someone else was being dragged up, probably whoever hadn't screamed loud enough for her death. The mob needed blood, and it wasn't particular about whose.

The guillotine blade sang its rainbow song, and somewhere, Queen Heartless was touching up her lipstick for the next performance.

But Alice didn't look back.

She couldn't afford to.

In this place, looking back was just another way to lose your head.

Chapter 7

Escape from Queerland

A lice ran through the gap in the wall of thorns, her heart hammering against her ribs. Behind her, the garden erupted in chaos. Queen Heartless shrieking orders, the mob turning on itself, someone already being dragged to the rainbow guillotine for the crime of insufficient enthusiasm.

She found herself in a strange in-between place. Not quite the garden, not quite the school. The walls seemed to be made of both stone and thought, shifting between solid and ethereal. The air tasted like lavender and chalk dust. Colors bled together like watercolors in rain. She could hear whispers, fragments of all the slogans and chants and accusations, but broken now, overlapping into meaninglessness.

"Well," a familiar voice said. "That was entertaining."

The Cheshire Cat sat on what might have been a rock or might have been a memory of a desk, fully visible, tail swishing. No fading in and out now. Just a cat, if cats could grin like they knew every secret in the world.

"You," Alice gasped, still catching her breath. "Where are we?"

"Between," the Cat replied. "This is where their world meets yours. Or where yours meets theirs. Depending on how you look at it. Dangerous place to be."

Alice leaned against a wall that felt both real and not. Her legs were still shaking from the run, from the near-execution, from everything she'd witnessed. "I learned what happens when people are so desperate to be good that they'll destroy anyone who makes them think."

"Close," the Cat said, dropping down to walk beside her. "You learned what happens when being right matters more than being human. When the performance becomes more important than the people."

"The mob turned on each other the second I escaped."

"They always do. That's the beautiful horror of it. They need enemies, and when they run out, they create them." The Cat began walking, and Alice followed through the shifting space. "Come. You need to get back before they notice how long you've been gone."

"How long have I been gone?"

"Time is funny here. Long enough to learn. Short enough that they can convince you it never happened, if you let them."

They walked through the in-between, the space gradually becoming more solid, more school-like. The Cat led with confidence, occasionally pausing as if listening to something Alice couldn't hear.

"The garden," Alice said. "Those heads. They just kept apologizing."

"Even after death, they couldn't stop performing. That's what happens when you apologize for existing. You forget how to do anything else." The Cat glanced back at her. "You didn't apologize."

"They wanted me to confess to thoughtcrimes. To admit that asking questions was violence."

"And you said no." The Cat's grin widened. "Do you understand how rare that is? Most people break. Most people decide it's easier to play along, to perform their assigned role. Most people would rather be headless than friendless."

They were climbing now, though Alice couldn't see stairs. Just an upward movement through space that was becoming increasingly familiar. The smell of industrial cleaner creeping in, the distant sound of bells and announcements.

"I mean," the Cat said, its form beginning to shimmer slightly, "that the question isn't whether you can escape Queerland. It's whether Queerland has already escaped into your world."

Alice felt a chill. "What do you mean?"

"Where do you think those ideas came from? The pronouns, the cancellations, the endless apologizing? They didn't invent them. They just...concentrated them. Showed you what they look like when they bloom. Showed you the garden they're planting, one apology at a time."

They reached what looked like a door, though it was more of a threshold between states of being. On the other side, Alice could see fluorescent lights, linoleum floors, the mundane reality of her school.

"Remember what you saw," the Cat said. "Remember that their power only exists if you play their game. There are other students starting to ask questions, you know. You're not as alone as they want you to think."

"Will I see you again?"

The Cat tilted its head. "I'm always around. Wherever someone asks a real question. Wherever someone says no to the mob. Wherever someone remembers that words mean things." It sat, tail curled around its feet. "The question is: what will you do with what you've learned?"

Alice opened her mouth to respond, but the cat had already lost interest. It stood, stretched lazily, and turned and walked away like it had something more important to do which, in the cat's opinion, was probably true.

Alice stepped through the threshold and found herself in a familiar hallway. Behind her, the door, or whatever it had been, was gone. Just a wall. A normal wall in a normal school where abnormal things were becoming mandatory.

The Reflection Suite was just around the corner. She could hear voices from inside. Taylor's professional concern, someone else's muffled responses. Another student being processed.

She walked to the Suite and opened the door.

Taylor looked up from their clipboard, relief flooding their face. "Alice! There you are. I've been looking everywhere. Where did you go?"

The other student, a boy Alice recognized from math class, sat in the chair she'd occupied. He looked small, scared, confused. A worksheet titled "Examining My Privileges" sat in his lap.

"I needed air," Alice said.

Taylor frowned. "You can't just leave. We have procedures. The workshop started fifteen minutes ago. Mx. Prism is already teaching. You've missed the introduction to fluid identity."

"I'm not going."

The words hung in the air. The boy in the chair looked up, surprised. Taylor's expression cycled through confusion, concern, and landed on professional disappointment.

"Alice, we've discussed this. The workshop is mandatory. After your incident in class, you need to show that you're willing to learn."

"No."

Taylor set down their clipboard. "I don't think you understand the seriousness of this. If you refuse processing, I'll have to escalate. Your parents will be called. The administration will get involved. Your teachers will be notified that you're refusing to address your harmful behavior."

"I asked what a woman is. That's not harmful. That's not violent. That's a question." Alice met Taylor's eyes. "And I won't pretend otherwise."

"This is exactly the kind of thinking that requires intervention."

"Then intervene. Call my parents. File your reports. Schedule your meetings." Alice moved toward the door. "I've seen where this leads. I've seen what happens to people who apologize for thinking. I won't be one of them."

Taylor stood, reaching for their phone. "If you leave now, I'll have to report this as a safety concern. You're exhibiting signs of radicalization."

"I'm exhibiting signs of thinking for myself. I know that terrifies you."

She left Taylor scrambling for protocols, the other student watching with wide eyes. In the hallway, she could already hear the machinery starting. Taylor's urgent phone call, the coded language about "intervention" and "safety" and "community standards."

Alice walked through the school with new eyes. She saw the posters differently now, not cheerful reminders but warnings. She saw the students differently, not just her peers but people performing their assigned roles, terrified of stepping wrong. She saw the fear beneath the smiles, the exhaustion beneath the enthusiasm, the desperate compliance masquerading as virtue.

Her phone buzzed. Dinah: "taylor says ur having a crisis. where r u?"

Then another: "everyones saying ur dangerous"

Then: "im worried about u"

Alice turned off her phone. She walked past the cafeteria where students were segregating themselves into approved identity groups. Past the library where books were being removed for "safety." Past the counseling office where someone was probably already preparing her file.

She pushed through the main doors into afternoon sunlight. Behind her, the building hummed with the business of control. Meetings being scheduled, parents being called, plans being made to fix her, save her, process her into compliance.

But Alice kept walking. She thought of the severed heads in the garden, apologizing forever. She thought of the shape-shifters who'd lost themselves in endless change. She thought of the academics drunk on their own theories. She thought of the Queen and her rainbow guillotine, performing justice as theater.

Real or not, she had seen the truth. The endpoint of the ideology. The world they were building, one apology at a time.

A car pulled up beside her. Her mother, face tight with worry and anger.

"Get in," she said. "The school called. We need to talk."

Alice got in. The lecture started before they'd left the parking lot. Disappointment. Concern. Embarrassment. The meeting tomorrow. The sessions they'd scheduled. The importance of community. The danger of isolation. The need to be better.

But Alice had been to the garden. She had seen the heads. And she would not apologize.

That night, she sat at her desk while her parents argued downstairs. Her father wanted to fight the school. Her mother wanted to comply. Neither asked what Alice wanted.

She pulled out her notebook and wrote:

"My name is Alice. I asked a question. I saw where silence leads. I choose to speak."

Tomorrow would bring new battles. New attempts to break her down. New isolation, new pressure, new promises that compliance would bring peace.

But Alice had learned something in that strange journey through the looking glass of ideology. She had learned that their reality was as fragile as they claimed hers was. That it required constant maintenance, constant performance, constant submission.

And she had learned the power of a simple word:

No.

It wasn't much against an entire system.

But it was a beginning.

And in her window, though she didn't see it, a cat-shaped shadow sat watching. Grinning. Waiting to see what questions she would ask tomorrow.

Epilogue

T he next day, Alice returned to school. Not because she wanted to, but because her parents made her. There had been phone calls. Concerns. Discussions about her "wellbeing."

The hallways buzzed with whispers. Her classmates looked at her differently, some with fear, some with anger, some with something that might have been envy. Word had spread about her refusal to be processed, her walking out, her "violent rejection of community standards."

She sat in history class as Mx. Peterson talked about World War I through a lens of "intersectional imperialism." No one asked questions. No one raised their hands. The lesson droned on, unopposed, unchallenged.

At lunch, she sat alone. Dinah wouldn't make eye contact. When Alice tried to approach, Dinah's new friends formed a protective barrier.

"She's not safe," one of them said loudly. "She literally commits violence by existing."

Alice ate in silence, watching her former friend perform her allyship, watching the others nod and validate and affirm. Dinah's eyes were glazed, distant. Happy.

Her phone buzzed. An email from the administration: "Mandatory Restorative Justice Circle - Tomorrow 3PM. Non-attendance will be considered an act of violence against the community."

Then another: "Alice, your teachers have expressed concern about your recent disengagement. We've scheduled you for intensive identity counseling starting Monday."

And another: "Your parents have been invited to a workshop on 'Supporting Your Problematic Child.' Their attendance is strongly encouraged."

The walls were closing in. Every day would bring new meetings, new sessions, new attempts to break her down. They would never stop. They couldn't stop. The system required her compliance.

But Alice had seen what compliance looked like. Rows of severed heads, still apologizing. Dinah's empty eyes. The faceless figure who had forgotten their own name.

She looked around the cafeteria. How many of these students were already gone? How many were just performing their assigned roles, their real selves buried under layers of approved identity? How many would end up like the heads in the garden, apologizing forever for the crime of having been themselves?

Most of them, probably. Maybe all of them, eventually.

Except her.

That night, Alice sat at her desk, staring at a blank notebook. Tomorrow they would try again. And the day after. And the day after that. They would never stop trying to process her, fix her, make her comply.

She picked up her pen and wrote:

"My name is Alice. I am thirteen years old. I asked what a woman is. I will not apologize."

She tore out the page and taped it to her mirror. A reminder. A declaration. A small act of resistance in a world that demanded surrender.

Outside her window, the world went on. Somewhere, committees were meeting to discuss her case. Somewhere, new protocols were being written to prevent another "Alice incident." Somewhere, her classmates were updating their bios, attending their workshops, disappearing into their performances.

But in her room, Alice remained Alice.

It wasn't much. But it was everything.

Because in a world where reality itself was being rewritten, remembering who you were became an act of revolution.

And forgetting became the only unforgivable sin.

The next morning, she would wake up and face it all again. The pressure. The isolation. The constant attempts to make her doubt herself. Most people couldn't withstand it forever. Most people broke, eventually.

But not today.

Today, she was still Alice.

And that had to be enough.

www.ingramcontent.com/pod-product-compliance
Lightning Source LLC
Chambersburg PA
CBHW061526020726
47502CB00006B/2252